J.K. Rowling

Bryan Pezzi

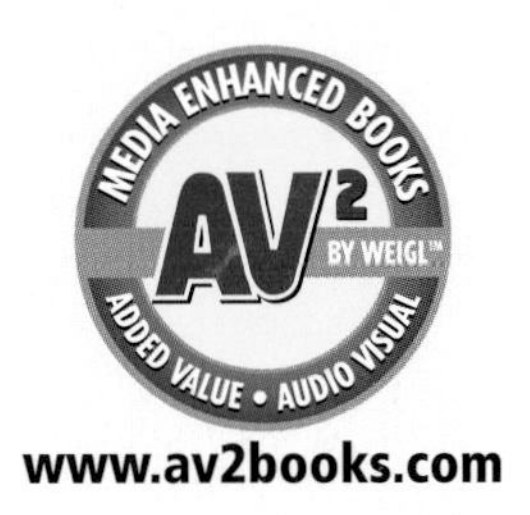

www.av2books.com

Go to **www.av2books.com**, and enter this book's unique code.

BOOK CODE

K503013

AV² by Weigl brings you media enhanced books that support active learning.

AV² provides enriched content that supplements and complements this book. Weigl's AV² books strive to create inspired learning and engage young minds in a total learning experience.

Your AV² Media Enhanced books come alive with...

Audio
Listen to sections of the book read aloud.

Key Words
Study vocabulary, and complete a matching word activity.

Video
Watch informative video clips.

Quizzes
Test your knowledge.

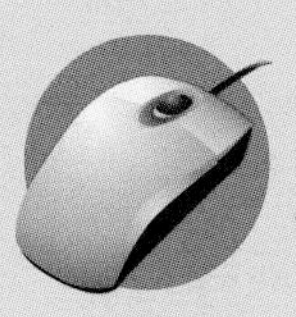

Embedded Weblinks
Gain additional information for research.

Slide Show
View images and captions, and prepare a presentation.

Try This!
Complete activities and hands-on experiments.

... and much, much more!

Published by AV² by Weigl
350 5th Avenue, 59th Floor
New York, NY 10118
Website: www.weigl.com www.av2books.com

Library of Congress Cataloging-in-Publication Data

Pezzi, Bryan.
J.K. Rowling / Bryan Pezzi.
p. cm. -- (Remarkable writers)
Includes index.
ISBN 978-1-61913-057-9 (hard cover : alk. paper) -- ISBN 978-1-61913-596-3 (soft cover : alk. paper) -- ISBN 978-1-61913-719-6 (ebook)
1. Rowling, J. K.--Juvenile literature. 2. Authors, English--20th century--Biography--Juvenile literature. 3. Children's stories--Authorship--Juvenile literature. 4. Potter, Harry (Fictitious character)--Juvenile literature. I. Title.
PR6068.O93Z825 2013
823'.914--dc23
[B]

2012003165

Printed in the United States of America in North Mankato, Minnesota
1 2 3 4 5 6 7 8 9 0 16 15 14 13 12

062012
WEP170512

Senior Editor: Heather Kissock
Designer: Terry Paulhus

Weigl acknowledges Getty Images as its primary photo supplier for this title.
Bloomsbury: pages 5 (Jason Cockcroft), 18 (Thomas Taylor), 21 (Jason Cockcroft); Raincoast Books: pages 5 (Cliff Wright, Michelle Radford, Giles Greenfield, Richard Horne), 13 (Cliff Wright, Michelle Radford), 19 (Cliff Wright, Michelle Radford), 20 (Cliff Wright), 21 (Giles Greenfield, Richard Horne).

Contents

Introducing J.K. Rowling

Joanne Kathleen (J.K.) Rowling has brought magic to millions of people. In the mid-1990s, she was a single mother struggling to publish her first novel. Today, she is a celebrity with fans around the world. The adventures of Harry Potter, a young boy with round glasses and a lightning-bolt scar on his forehead, have made her famous.

Harry Potter appeared in 1997 when Joanne's first novel, *Harry Potter and the Philosopher's Stone*, was published in Great Britain. The book tells the story of an orphan named Harry, who does not know he is a wizard. Harry discovers a world of magic and wonder when he attends Hogwarts School. There, he studies magic with his new friends, Ron Weasley and Hermione Granger.

Due to the success of the Harry Potter series, J.K. Rowling is now one of the world's best-known children's authors.

No other children's writer has achieved the same success as Joanne. More than a quarter of a billion Harry Potter books have been sold worldwide. Translated into 61 languages, the books are sold in more than 200 countries.

J.K. Rowling enjoys meeting her fans and speaking with them about her books.

Writing A Biography

Writers are often inspired to record the stories of people who lead interesting lives. The story of another person's life is known as a biography. A biography can tell the story of any person, from authors such as J.K. Rowling, to inventors, presidents, and sports stars.

When writing a biography, authors must first collect information about their subject. This information may come from a book about the person's life, a news article about one of his or her accomplishments, or a review of his or her work. Libraries and the internet will have much of this information. Most biographers will also interview their subjects. Personal accounts provide a great deal of information and a unique point of view. When some basic details about the person's life have been collected, it is time to begin writing a biography.

As you read about J.K. Rowling, you will be introduced to the important parts of a biography. Use these tips, and the examples provided, to learn how to write about an author or any other remarkable person.

Early Life

Joanne Rowling was born on July 31, 1965. Joanne's father, Peter, was an engineer, and her mother, Anne, was a **lab technician**. In 1967, Joanne's sister, Diana, was born. The family lived in the town of Chipping Sodbury in western England. When Joanne was four years old, the family moved to Winterbourne. Winterbourne is near Bristol in southwestern England.

"The small amount of time that we didn't spend fighting, Di and I were best friends. I told her a lot of stories and sometimes didn't even have to sit on her to make her stay and listen."
—J.K. Rowling

As a young girl, Joanne was known as "Jo" to her family. Diana was called "Di." Joanne was short and round, and wore very thick glasses. She was the "bright one" in the family, while her sister Di was the "pretty one." Neither girl liked these labels. Joanne was bossy with her sister, but she was shy with strangers. Joanne and her sister often argued.

Winterbourne is a village with a population of about 8,500.

Although they fought, Joanne and Di were best friends. They enjoyed playing together. Joanne invented plays and skits, and Di acted in them. The girls never tired of these dramas. One of their favorite **scenarios** to act out was for one girl to cling to the other girl's hand, pretending she was dangling from a cliff. The girls were actually sitting at the top of the stairs. The dangling girl would pretend she was going to fall from a cliff, and would beg her sister to hold her. The scenario always ended with the dangling girl pretending to fall to her doom.

Joanne also enjoyed making up stories. Sometimes, she invented tales to entertain her sister. Soon, she began writing her stories down on paper. Joanne wrote her first book when she was 6 years old. It was a story about a bunny named Rabbit. In her story, Rabbit caught the **measles**. All of Rabbit's friends came to visit him. One of his friends was an insect named Miss Bee. Joanne was proud of her first book.

Writing About Early Life

A person's early years have a strong influence on his or her future. Parents, teachers, and friends can have a large impact on how a person thinks, feels, and behaves. These effects are strong enough to last throughout childhood, and often a person's lifetime.

In order to write about a person's early life, biographers must find answers to the following questions.

1. Where and when was the person born?
2. What is known about the person's family and friends?
3. Did the person grow up in unusual circumstances?

Children often dress up and stage plays for family members and friends.

Growing Up

Joanne enjoyed school in Winterbourne, especially drawing and pottery. Joanne was happiest when she was reading and writing. After school, Joanne played with her sister or with friends. Sometimes she played with a brother and sister with the last name of Potter.

Joanne liked the name Potter. She preferred it to her own name, Rowling, which is pronounced "rolling." This name lead to jokes like "Rowling stone" and "Rowling pin."

"When I was quite young, my parents never said books were off limits."
—J.K. Rowling

Around the time of her ninth birthday, Joanne's family moved to Tutshill, a small village in Wales. This was not a happy time for Joanne. Not only did she have to move to a new home, but her favorite grandparent, Kathleen, died. Joanne was very sad about the death of her grandmother. She later took her grandmother's name as her own middle name.

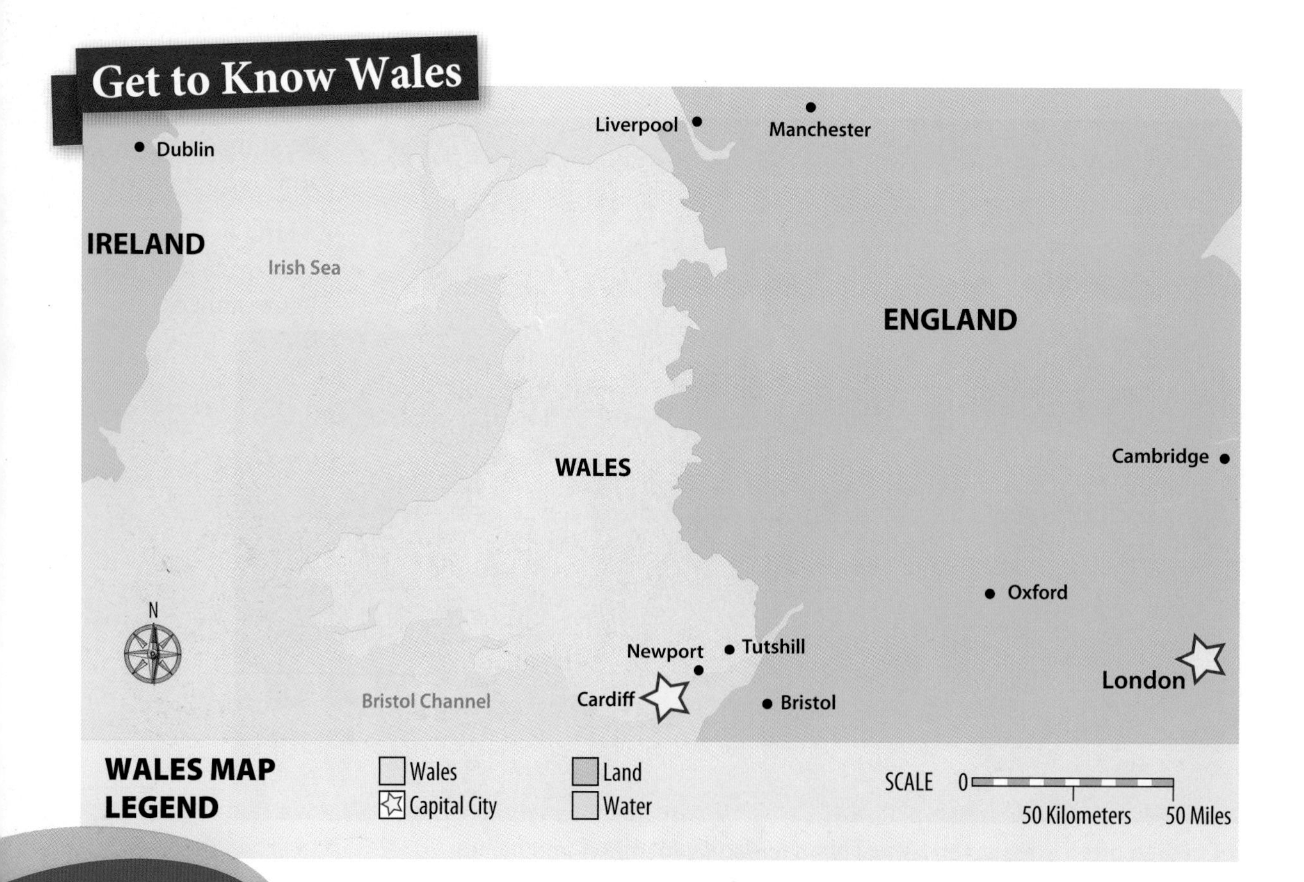

Joanne found it difficult to adjust to her new school. She did not like the school. On her first day of classes, Joanne failed a math test because she had not learned fractions. As punishment, her teacher sat her in the row reserved for students who did poorly. Joanne worked very hard to earn higher grades. By the end of the year, she was able to sit with the better students.

Joanne grew happier when she entered secondary school at 11 years of age. Here she met Sean Harris, who became one of her best friends. Sean supported Joanne's goal to be a writer. Joanne says Sean was similar to the character of Ron Weasley in the Harry Potter books. Joanne was more like Hermione Granger. She was shy, bookish, and a worrywart. As teenagers, Joanne and Sean took rides in Sean's car. This was Joanne's first taste of freedom and her happiest teenage memory.

Writing About Growing Up

Some people know what they want to achieve in life from a very young age. Others do not decide until much later. In any case, it is important for biographers to discuss when and how their subjects make these decisions. Using the information they collect, biographers try to answer the following questions about their subjects' paths in life.

1. Who had the most influence on the person?
2. Did he or she receive assistance from others?
3. Did the person have a positive attitude?

In the Harry Potter movies, Rupert Grint plays Ron Weasley, and Emma Watson plays Hermione Granger.

Developing Skills

When Joanne was 15, her mother, Anne, was diagnosed with multiple sclerosis (MS). This disease attacks the **central nervous system**. It can cause **paralysis** and blindness. Some people with MS experience periods of **remission**. Their disease may stop progressing or they may begin recovering for a while. Unfortunately, this did not happen for Joanne's mother. Her illness grew steadily worse. This was a difficult time for Joanne. It was hard for Joanne to watch her mother's health fail.

"It's important to remember that we all have magic inside us."
—J.K. Rowling

In 1983, Joanne graduated with honors from Wyedean Comprehensive School. She wanted to enroll in Oxford University, but she was not accepted. Instead, Joanne enrolled at the University of Exeter, on the southern coast of England. She studied French and **Classics**. The best part of Joanne's French education was spending a year in Paris, France.

The University of Exeter was founded in 1950. It is considered one of England's top universities.

After graduating from university, Joanne moved to London, England. She worked as a secretary, but found that she did not enjoy **clerical** work much. Joanne said she was disorganized. She also found it difficult to pay attention in meetings. Instead of paying attention and taking detailed notes, Joanne often wrote story ideas. When no one was looking, she wrote stories on her computer. Joanne wanted to write. She found clerical work boring. Joanne also worked as a researcher for Amnesty International. Amnesty International is an organization that promotes and protects **human rights** around the world. Joanne worked at this job longer than any other.

While in Paris, Joanne worked as a teacher's assistant. In Paris, she saw many famous landmarks, including the Eiffel Tower.

Writing About Developing Skills

Every remarkable person has skills and traits that make him or her noteworthy. Some people have natural talent, while others practice diligently. For most, it is a combination of the two. One of the most important things that a biographer can do is to tell the story of how their subject developed his or her talents.

1. What was the person's education?
2. What was the person's first job or work experience?
3. What obstacles did the person overcome?

Timeline of J.K. Rowling

1965

Joanne Rowling is born on July 31 in Chipping Sodbury, England. The family later moved to the town of Winterbourne, in southwest England.

1987

Joanne graduates from the University of Exeter, where she studied French and Classics.

1990

After living in London, England for a few years, Joanne moves to Manchester. It is here that she begins writing a story about a young wizard named Harry Potter.

1991

Following the death of her mother, Joanne moves to Oporto, Portugal, to teach English.

1994

Joanne returns to Great Britain with her daughter. They settle in Edinburgh, Scotland.

1995
Joanne completes the first Harry Potter book. She hires a **literary agent** to help her get the book published.

1997
Harry Potter and the Philosopher's Stone is published in Great Britain. It wins several awards, including the Children's Book of the Year at the British Book Awards.

1998
Harry Potter and the Chamber of Secrets is published and wins the Nestlé Smarties Book Prize.

2000
Harry Potter and the Goblet of Fire becomes the fastest-selling book in history.

2001
The first Harry Potter movie appears in theaters.

Early Achievements

In 1990, Joanne moved to Manchester, England. On a crowded train from Manchester to London, the idea for Harry Potter first popped into her head. While the train was delayed, Joanne imagined a scrawny, black-haired boy with glasses. He had magical powers but did not know he was a wizard. Harry Potter grew more and more real to Joanne. She imagined Harry's lightning-bolt scar and Hogwarts School, along with many of Harry's teachers and classmates. Joanne did not have a pen and was too shy to ask to borrow one. She used her imagination and tried to remember the details so that she could write them down later.

"It is impossible to live without failing at something, unless you live so cautiously that you might as well not have lived at all—in which case, you fail by default."
—J.K. Rowling

That night, Joanne began writing her first Harry Potter novel. Over the next few months, the **manuscript** grew. Joanne also wrote down ideas for other books in the series.

That same year, something happened to greatly change Joanne's life. Her mother, Anne, died at the age of 45. It was a terrible time for Joanne, her sister, and their father. They never imagined that Anne would die so young. After this terrible event, Joanne was desperate to move away.

In the Harry Potter books, the main characters attend Hogwarts School of Witchcraft and Wizardry. It is here that they learn the theory and skills needed to perform magic. The school has been recreated at an amusement park in Florida.

Joanne moved to Portugal and found a job teaching English. She continued to work on her novel. The book changed after Joanne's mother died. Harry's feelings toward his dead parents became much deeper and more real. During Joanne's first weeks in Portugal, she wrote her favorite chapter of the book. It is called "The Mirror of Erised." In this chapter, Harry finds a magic mirror that reveals his deepest desire. Harry's greatest wish is to be with his parents.

While living in Portugal, Joanne married a Portuguese **journalist**. In 1993, Joanne gave birth to her daughter, Jessica. The marriage did not last. In 1994, Joanne returned to Great Britain with her young daughter. She had not finished writing her first novel.

Joanne taught English in Oporto, or Porto, Portugal. Porto is Portugal's second-largest city.

Writing About Early Achievements

No two people take the same path to success. Some people work very hard for a long time before achieving their goals. Others may take advantage of a fortunate turn of events. Biographers must make special note of the traits and qualities that allow their subjects to succeed.

1. What was the person's most important early success?
2. What process does the person use in his or her work?
3. Which of the person's traits were most helpful in his or her work?

Tricks of the Trade

Writing is difficult, but it can be very rewarding. J.K. Rowling has been working at her craft for many years. During that time, she has learned ways to make her writing better. Here are some tips that might help you write better.

Take Inspiration from Real Life

The Harry Potter books are works of fantasy, but many of the characters and ideas come from Joanne's life. Some characters have been inspired by friends or teachers Joanne knew as a girl. Are there any people, places, or situations in your life that might make a good story? You can base your writing on something real, and then add fictional ideas to it. By working your own magic, you can take real life and turn it into a great story.

Plan an Outline

Planning an outline can make writing much easier. Joanne always knows what will happen in one of her books before she sits down to write it. During the time Joanne wrote the first Harry Potter book, she was also planning the next six books in the series. After you plan your outline, think about the characters in your story.

Practice

Writing takes a great deal of practice. Joanne had to practice writing for many years before she became a successful author. She wrote many stories that were never published. Try to make time to write each day. It is also important to read as much as you can. Reading the work of successful writers will give you ideas to improve your own writing.

Rowling liked to write in cafés because the walk there would help her baby fall asleep.

Use Your Imagination and Have Fun

Joanne writes the kinds of stories she would like to read. She is a writer because it is the job that gives her the greatest enjoyment. Writing is hard work, but it should also be fun. Joanne creates characters and situations that are funny, silly, and outrageous. Fans of Harry Potter will remember when he accidentally blew up his nasty Aunt Marge. Remember when Hermione's potion backfired and turned her into a cat? Follow Joanne's example, and let your imagination run wild. You can write about things that are silly or totally unrealistic.

Remarkable Books

Although J.K. Rowling has written all her life, only the Harry Potter books have been published. Joanne wrote seven novels for the series. Each book tells about Harry's experiences during one year at Hogwarts School.

Harry Potter and the Sorcerer's Stone

Joanne's first book was published in Great Britain as *Harry Potter and the Philosopher's Stone*. In it, readers are introduced to the magical world of Harry Potter. Harry is 11 years old. He is an orphan living with his unloving relatives, the Dursleys.

One day, Harry receives a letter inviting him to attend Hogwarts School of Witchcraft and Wizardry. The letter changes his world forever. Harry discovers that his parents were wizards and that he has magical powers.

At Hogwarts School, Harry learns how to use his magical powers. He especially enjoys Quidditch, a sport played on broomsticks. Harry learns that a special jewel called the Sorcerer's Stone is hidden in Hogwarts School. The stone can give wealth and eternal life to the owner. Harry and his friends must perform daring feats to find the stone.

AWARDS
Harry Potter and the Sorcerer's Stone
1997 National Book Award (UK)
1998 Sheffield Children's Book Award

daring feats to find the stone.

Harry Potter and the Chamber of Secrets

At the beginning of this book, Dobby, a house elf, visits Harry. Dobby warns that Harry is in danger and should not return to Hogwarts School. Harry decides to return to school anyway. When Harry and his friend, Ron, try to board the train to Hogwarts, they are unable to enter the magic train platform. The two friends must fly in a magic car to get to school.

At Hogwarts, the students have a new professor, Gilderoy Lockhart. He is **vain** and boastful. He is also a constant annoyance to Harry.

Strange things begin to happen at Hogwarts. A threatening message is written on a school wall. Students mysteriously turn to stone. People become suspicious of Harry when they learn he has the ability to speak to snakes. Things become more serious when Ron's sister, Ginny, is kidnapped. Harry, Ron, and Hermione are determined to solve the mystery. Together they search for a secret chamber hidden in the castle. Inside the chamber, they must face terrible dangers and bring Ginny back to safety.

AWARDS
Harry Potter and the Chamber of Secrets
1998 Nestlé Smarties Prize
1998 British Children's Book Award
1998 New York Public Library Best Book of the Year

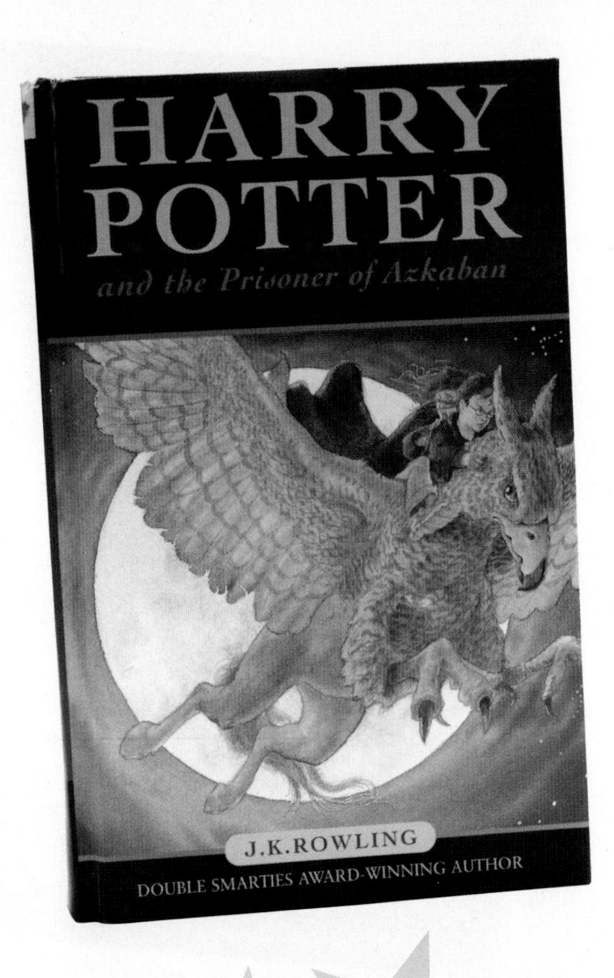

Harry Potter and the Prisoner of Azkaban

The wizarding world is shocked when a dangerous murderer escapes from Azkaban Prison. Sirius Black, a dark wizard, is on the loose. Now in his third year at Hogwarts School, Harry Potter's life is in danger. When Harry was a baby, Black helped Lord Voldemort kill Harry's parents. Now, Harry fears that Black will find him and murder him, too.

Frightening monsters called dementors are stationed around Hogwarts to guard the school. The dementors are so frightening that Harry faints whenever one comes near. Harry's new Defense Against Dark Arts teacher, Professor Lupin, helps him overcome his fears and unlock the secrets of his past. Hogwarts School is on high alert when an unseen intruder enters the castle. Eventually Harry, Ron, and Hermione must face the escaped wizard.

AWARDS
Harry Potter and the Prisoner of Azkaban
1999 Nestlé Smarties Prize
1999 Whitbread Children's Book of the Year Award
1999 Bram Stoker Award
2000 Locus Poll Award

Harry Potter and the Goblet of Fire

When Harry returns for his fourth year at Hogwarts, the school is full of excitement. Hogwarts will host an international event called the Triwizard Tournament. Three students will compete in the tournament.

On Halloween night, the Goblet reveals the names of the three champions who will compete in the tournament. Everyone is shocked when the Goblet also reveals a fourth name—Harry Potter. Harry is too young and does not want to compete, but the Goblet's decision is final. Aside from the tournament, Harry must face an even more dangerous threat—Lord Voldemort.

Harry Potter and the Order of the Phoenix

Evil Lord Voldemort has returned to the wizarding world. Harry Potter knows that Voldemort is a terrible threat, but few people believe Harry. However, a group of wizards believes Harry and forms the Order of the Phoenix to fight Voldemort.

At Hogwarts School, the Ministry of Magic has sent an official to take control of the school. Delores Umbridge is the new High Inquisitor of Hogwarts. Umbridge dislikes Harry because she believes Harry tells lies about Lord Voldemort.

AWARDS
Harry Potter and the Order of the Phoenix
2003 Bram Stoker Award

Umbridge's punishments, year-end exams, and terrifying nightmares all make Harry's fifth year especially difficult. Harry and his friends form a club and learn how to protect themselves from dark magic. Soon, they must confront Lord Voldemort and his evil servants.

From Big Ideas to Books

When Joanne and her daughter left Portugal, they moved to Edinburgh, Scotland, where Joanne's sister was living. At first, life in Edinburgh was difficult for Joanne. She was a single parent living in poor conditions. Joanne applied for **welfare** to support herself and her daughter. Sometimes she found secretarial work for a few hours a week. Joanne intended to start teaching again, but this idea worried her. She did not think she would have time to finish her book if she taught school and cared for Jessica.

"I'm very selfish; I just write for me. So the humor in the books is really what I find funny."
—J. K. Rowling

Joanne put all of her energy into finishing her novel. She worked on her book every evening. After Jessica fell asleep, Joanne wrote. During this time, she did all of her writing with a pen and paper. Joanne did not have a typewriter or a computer.

Finishing the book was difficult for Joanne. Sometimes she hated the book, and sometimes she became depressed. Still, Joanne had a good story and characters that she loved.

The Publishing Process

Publishing companies receive hundreds of manuscripts from authors each year. Only a few manuscripts become books. Publishers must be sure that a manuscript will sell many copies. As a result, publishers reject most of the manuscripts they receive. Once a manuscript has been accepted, it goes through

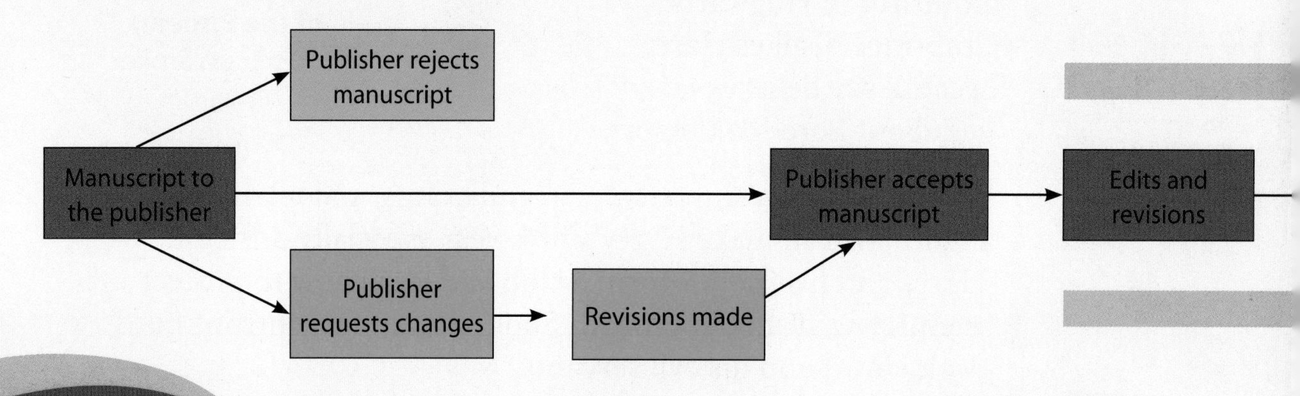

Joanne's sister, Di, was the first person with whom Joanne shared her story. Di liked Harry Potter and encouraged her sister to continue writing. Joanne applied for a writing **grant** through the Scottish Arts Council. They awarded her some money, which allowed her to finish writing the book.

In 1995, Joanne finished her novel. She bought an old typewriter and prepared several manuscripts. Now, Joanne needed an agent to help sell her work to a publishing company. She sent the first three chapters of her book to an agent. This agent rejected Joanne's idea. The second agent Joanne contacted was more interested. His name was Christopher Little. He wanted to read the rest of Joanne's manuscript.

Together, Joanne and Christopher searched for a company to publish Harry Potter. In August 1996, Christopher phoned Joanne to tell her that Bloomsbury Publishing would publish her book. After many years of work, Harry Potter would finally be published.

The final book in the series, *Harry Potter and the Deathly Hallows,* was published in 2007.

many stages before it is published. Often, authors change their work to follow an editor's suggestions. Once the book is published, some authors receive royalties. This is money based on book sales.

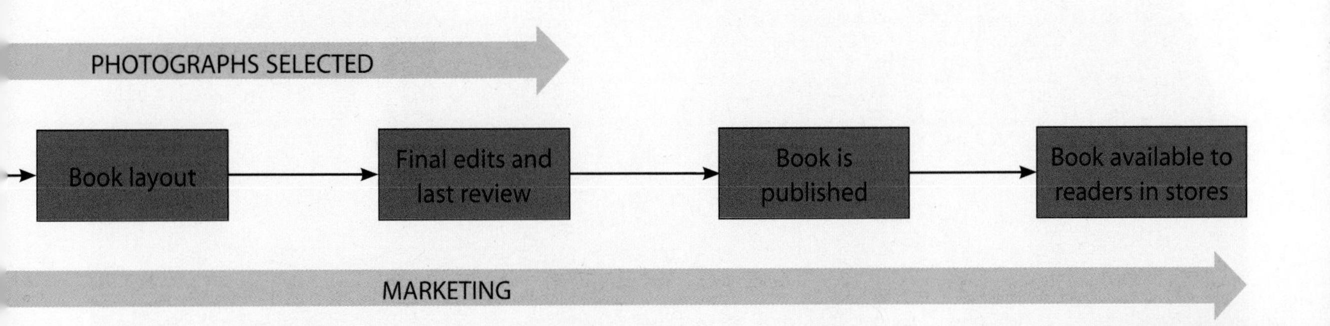

J.K. Rowling Today

Today, J. K. Rowling is one of the most popular writers in the world. Bloomsbury Publishing released *Harry Potter and the Philosopher's Stone* in Great Britain in 1997. The next year, Scholastic Books published Joanne's novel in the United States. Joanne's publishers suggested that she use her initials rather than the name Joanne. They thought boys might not want to read the book if they knew a woman wrote it. Joanne used the middle initial, "K," to represent her grandmother, Kathleen.

Joanne's first novel received good reviews. Readers thought the book was imaginative and funny. Children and many adults liked *Harry Potter and the Sorcerer's Stone*. They enjoyed reading about Harry, Ron, and Hermione, and their adventures at Hogwarts School.

The seven Harry Potter books were made into eight movies, with the final book made in two parts. Rupert Grint, Daniel Radcliffe, and Emma Watson starred in all eight of the Harry Potter movies.

With the success of her first book, Joanne's life improved. She bought a computer and used it to finish her second book, *Harry Potter and the Chamber of Secrets.*

By the time Joanne finished her fourth Harry Potter book, she was a superstar. *Harry Potter and the Goblet of Fire* became the fastest-selling book in history. It was as long as her first three novels together. Readers loved it. The fifth book, *Harry Potter and the Order of the Phoenix,* was even longer—more than 700 pages.

When the first Harry Potter books were made into movies, Joanne was concerned that the films might not be faithful to the books. Fortunately, she worked closely with the filmmakers. The movies, like the books, have been incredibly successful.

Joanne loves writing. Her books have been published all over the world. She still lives in Scotland with her family. In December 2001, she married Dr. Neil Murray. Their son, David, was born in March 2003. Joanne wrote the sixth book in the Harry Potter series, *Harry Potter and the Half-Blood Prince,* while pregnant with her third child, daughter Mackenzie.

Writing About the Person Today

The biography of any living person is an ongoing story. People have new ideas, start new projects, and deal with challenges. For their work to be meaningful, biographers must include up-to-date information about their subjects. Through research, biographers try to answer the following questions.

1. Has the person received awards or recognition for accomplishments?
2. What is the person's life's work?
3. How have the person's accomplishments served others?

Since finishing the Harry Potter series, J.K. Rowling has been working on her first book for adults. *A Casual Vacancy* is scheduled to be published in 2012.

Fan Information

Readers all over the world love J.K. Rowling's books. Joanne loves to hear from her fans. Unfortunately, she receives so many letters that she cannot respond to them all. If she did, she would never have time to write her books.

Joanne enjoys making public appearances to read from her books. When the first Harry Potter book was released, Joanne read to small gatherings of just a few people. Today, a J.K. Rowling reading is a major event. Joanne reads to thousands of people all at once. At the SkyDome in Toronto, Canada, in 2000, Joanne read to more than 20,000 people. It is thought to be the world's largest book reading.

Pottermore is a website that Rowling has created to let users explore the world of Harry Potter in a fun, interactive way.

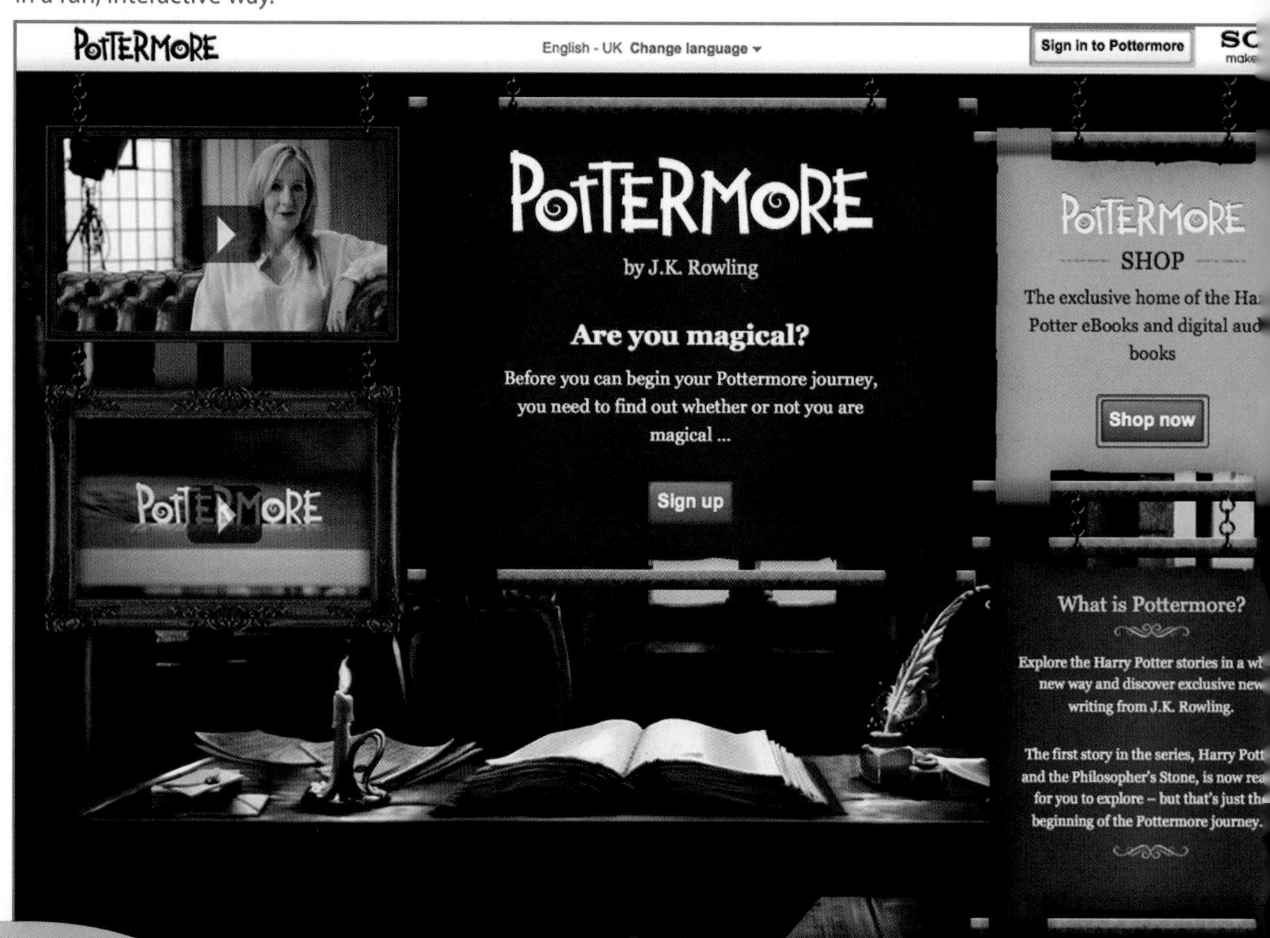

Another special reading took place in 2003. Joanne appeared before 4,000 fans at London's Royal Albert Hall. For this event, the hall was turned into Hogwarts School. There were moving portraits and ushers dressed as Hogwarts pupils. It is a sign that she has touched many people's lives with Harry Potter's magic. Joanne said at the 2008 Harvard Commencement Address that she is still nervous about speaking in public, but people are very enthusiastic about her appearances.

The Internet has thousands of websites devoted to J.K. Rowling and Harry Potter. Some of these are official sites created by publishers, movie studios, or Joanne herself. Other sites have been created by fans who want to share information about the books and connect with other readers. You may also find interviews with Joanne or news stories about Harry Potter events.

Write a Biography

All of the parts of a biography work together to tell the story of a person's life. Find out how these elements combine by writing a biography. Begin by choosing a person whose story fascinates you. You will have to research the person's life by using library books and the reliable websites. You can also email the person or write him or her a letter. The person might agree to answer your questions directly.

Use a concept web, such as the one below, to guide you in writing the biography. Answer each of the questions listed using the information you have gathered. Each heading on the concept web will form an important part of the person's story.

Parts of a Biography

Early Life

Where and when was the person born?

What is known about the person's family and friends?

Did the person grow up in unusual circumstances?

Growing Up

Who had the most influence on the person?

Did he or she receive assistance from others?

Did the person have a positive attitude?

Developing Skills

What was the person's education?

What was the person's first job or work experience?

What obstacles did the person overcome?

Early Achievements

What was the person's most important early success?

What processes does this person use in his or her work?

Which of the person's traits were most helpful in his or her work?

Person Today

Has the person received awards or recognition for accomplishments?

What is the person's life's work?

How have the person's accomplishments served others?

Test Yourself

1 Where and when was J.K. Rowling born?

2 Where did Joanne move to when she was nine years old?

3 What subjects did Joanne study at the University of Exeter?

4 Where was Joanne when she first imagined Harry Potter?

5 What country did Joanne move to after the death of her mother?

6 How many Harry Potter books did Joanne write?

7 Where is Joanne's favorite place to write?

8 What was *Harry Potter and the Sorcerer's Stone* called in Great Britain?

9 Where was Joanne's largest book reading?

10 What are the names of Harry Potter's two best friends?

ANSWERS

1. J.K. Rowling was born in Chipping Sodbury, England, in 1965. **2.** Tutshill, a village in Wales **3.** French and Classics **4.** On a crowded train from Manchester to London **5.** Portugal **6.** Seven **7.** She likes to write in cafés. **8.** *Harry Potter and the Philosopher's Stone* **9.** The Sky Dome in Toronto, Canada **10.** Ron Weasley and Hermione Granger.

Writing Terms

The field of writing has its own language. Understanding some of the more common writing terms will allow you to discuss your ideas about books.

action: the moving events of a work of fiction

antagonist: the person in the story who opposes the main character

autobiography: a history of a person's life written by that person

biography: a written account of another person's life

character: a person in a story, poem, or play

climax: the most exciting moment or turning point in a story

episode: a scene or short piece of action in a story

fiction: stories about characters and events that are not real

foreshadow: hinting at something that is going to happen later in the book

imagery: a written description of a thing or idea that brings an image to mind

narrator: the speaker of the story who relates the events

nonfiction: writing that deals with real people and events

novel: published writing of considerable length that portrays characters within a story

plot: the order of events in a work of fiction

protagonist: the leading character of a story; often a likable character

resolution: the end of the story, when the conflict is settled

scene: a single episode in a story

setting: the place and time in which a work of fiction occurs

theme: an idea that runs throughout a work of fiction

Key Words

central nervous system: the brain and spinal cord
Classics: literature of lasting significance
clerical: office work, such as filing and typing
grant: money awarded for a specific reason or cause
human rights: the basic freedoms to which all people are entitled, such as the right to food and shelter, freedom from slavery, and freedom to worship
journalist: a writer who works for a newspaper or magazine
lab technician: a person who analyzes chemical samples
literary agent: a person who works with an author to help get his or her books published
manuscript: draft of a story before it is published
measles: a childhood disease that causes a fever and a rash of red spots on the body
paralysis: the loss of movement or feeling in part of the body
remission: a period when a disease improves or stops progressing
scenarios: imagined sequences of possible events
vain: too proud of one's looks, abilities, or achievements
welfare: money given by the government to help people living in poverty

Index

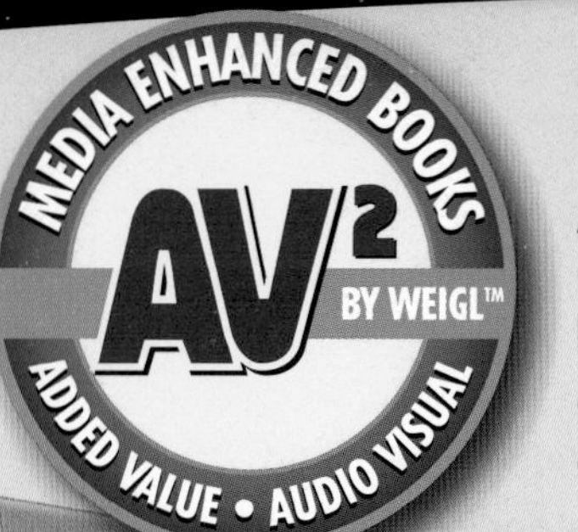

Log on to www.av2books.com

AV² by Weigl brings you media enhanced books that support active learning. Go to www.av2books.com, and enter the special code found on page 2 of this book. You will gain access to enriched and enhanced content that supplements and complements this book. Content includes video, audio, weblinks, quizzes, a slide show, and activities.

Audio
Listen to sections of the book read aloud.

Video
Watch informative video clips.

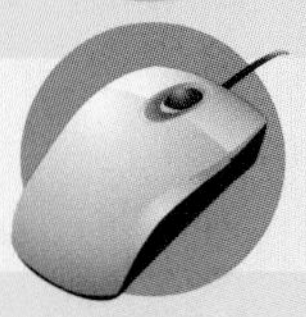

Embedded Weblinks
Gain additional information for research.

Try This!
Complete activities and hands-on experiments.

WHAT'S ONLINE?

Try This!

Complete an activity about your childhood.

Try this timeline activity.

See what you know about the publishing process.

Test your knowledge of writing terms.

Write a biography.

Embedded Weblinks

Learn more about J.K. Rowling's life.

Learn more about J.K. Rowling's achievements.

Check out this site about J.K. Rowling.

Video

Watch a video about J.K. Rowling.

Watch this interview with J.K. Rowling.

EXTRA FEATURES

Audio
Listen to sections of the book read aloud.

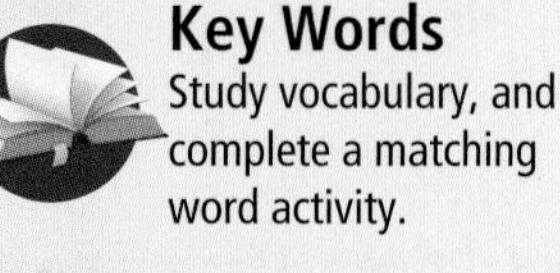

Key Words
Study vocabulary, and complete a matching word activity.

Slide Show
View images and captions, and prepare a presentation.

Quizzes
Test your knowledge.

AV² was built to bridge the gap between print and digital. We encourage you to tell us what you like and what you want to see in the future.

Sign up to be an AV² Ambassador at www.av2books.com/ambassador.

Due to the dynamic nature of the Internet, some of the URLs and activities provided as part of AV² by Weigl may have changed or ceased to exist. AV² by Weigl accepts no responsibility for any such changes. All media enhanced books are regularly monitored to update addresses and sites in a timely manner. Contact AV² by Weigl at 1-866-649-3445 or av2books@weigl.com with any questions, comments, or feedback.